Illustrated by Anthony Williams

Titles in Alien Detective Agency

Badger Publishing Limited
Suite G08,
Stevenage, Hertfordshire SG1 2DX
Telephone: 01438 791 037
Fax: 01438 791 036
www.badgerlearning.co.uk

Mirror, Mirror ISBN 978-1-84926-618-5

Publisher: Sus
Senior Editor:
Design: Julia
Illustration: A

Mirror, Mirror

Contents

Vocabulary:

monstrous – like a monster

belfry – a bell tower

inter-galactic

– travelling between galaxies in space

Martian – from the planet Mars

banshee – a spirit from Irish myths whose scream was very loud

Main characters:

Jack Swift – the star of a top rated TV show

Wanda Darkstar –

the Galactic Union's Alien Welfare Officer for Earth

Jar-Wob – an evil vampire from Venus

STEALTH – Jack's spaceship

Chapter 1
Reflecting

Jack was doing one of his favourite things. He was looking in the mirror – and rehearsing his lines.

Jack was a famous actor on the hit TV show 'Sci-Fi Spy Guy'.

He was practising a scene where he fought a nasty alien: "Your evil plans are all awry – you just messed with the wrong Spy Guy!" he announced.

But instead of the mirror echoing his words, it said, "Stop looking at yourself and listen to me!"

"Huh?" said Jack.

He looked in the mirror – but he didn't see his own face, he saw Wanda!

Wanda was his partner in their Alien Detective Agency.

Jack looked behind him, but Wanda wasn't there.

"Over here, Spy Guy!"

He looked back in the mirror. There was Wanda staring out at him. She looked really annoyed.

"What are you doing in my mirror?" he asked.

"That's a very good question," she replied. "I've been trapped in here since last night. I've been waiting for you to look in the mirror. I didn't think I'd have to wait so long!"

"But how did you get there?" asked Jack.

Wanda frowned. "I don't know how she did it, but Jar-Wob, that evil alien from Venus, put me here. You've got to get me out."

"How?" said Jack.

"I don't know," said Wanda, "but she is going to be in trouble when I catch up with her. You have to make her put me back."

"Where is she now?" asked Jack.

"She lives on the planet Venus. Don't let her get too close to you – she's dangerous near humans," said Wanda seriously.

"Why?" Jack asked.

"Because she's a vampire," said Wanda.

"What a pain in the neck," said Jack.

Chapter 2

The dark side of Venus

Jack went to get his spaceship, STEALTH.

He kept it at the TV studio because everyone thought it was a pretend spaceship. Only he and Wanda knew the truth. Or so he thought.

"Come on, STEALTH," he said. "We have a damsel in distress!"

"Less of the 'damsel' stuff," said a muffled voice.

"Huh?" said Jack.

He got a small mirror out of his pocket. There was Wanda in the mirror.

"It's hot and stuffy in your pocket," she said.

Jack rolled his eyes. "How did you get in there?"

Wanda grinned. "Every mirror you look in, you'll see me."

Jack groaned. As if he didn't have enough problems. He shoved the mirror back in his pocket.

"Hey!" said a muffled voice. But Jack ignored it.

It didn't take long for STEALTH to fly to Venus.

Jack looked down at the dry, yellow planet. He couldn't see any water, just miles and miles of sand dunes.

"Head for the dark side," hissed Wanda.

STEALTH swooped round the planet, passing from day to dusk to night.

"Now which way?" asked Jack, opening the mirror again.

"Head for Dracula's Castle!" said Wanda.

Jack thought Wanda was joking, but then STEALTH's monitors picked up a large, stone building. It rose up out of the dark desert, monstrous and evil, but beautiful, too.

STEALTH landed with a soft thump.

"Watch your back, Jack," said Wanda.

There was only one way into the castle – through a huge, heavy wooden door. When Jack pushed, it creaked loudly.

"Nice going, Spy Guy," muttered Wanda. "That was loud enough to wake the dead."

"Yes, it was!" said a chilling voice.

Chapter 3
A lot at stake

"Welcome to my lair, I mean, home," said the vampire. "I am Jar-Wob. Pleased to eat you, I mean, meet you."

The vampire was tall and thin with long green hair and teeth like piano keys.

Instead of hands she had claws. When she smiled it was like watching a hedgehog cross a motorway.

"You may be cool for a ghoul," said Jack, "but there's too much at stake to let you go."

Jack held a long, sharp stick in front of him.

Jar-Wob threw back her head and laughed like a bottle full of drain cleaner. "If you think that's going to stop me, you're myth-taken! Ha ha ha!"

"Use my laser!" bawled Wanda from Jack's pocket.

"I left it on STEALTH," he hissed.

"Oh dear, my dear!" cackled Jar-Wob.

"You're going from bad to worse to curse!"

She held out a mirror and pointed her long, yellow nails at it.

Jack didn't know what to do – but Wanda did. "Run!" she yelled.

Jack took to his toes before Jar-Wob could curse him into the mirror.

He ran faster than a lunar mouse after a cat.

Jar-Wob kept throwing curses at him. Luckily they all missed, but a pair of heavy curtains vanished into the mirror along with a lumpy old sofa.

"Ouch!" said Wanda, as the curtains landed on her head and she fell backwards onto the sofa. It was getting pretty crowded in the mirror.

Jack dived through a door and looked around him. There was no way out!

They were trapped!

"Nice try, Spy Guy," muttered Wanda.

It all went quiet.

"I think I've got her on the run!" whispered Jack.

At that moment they heard STEALTH's engines start.

Suddenly Jack realised what Jar-Wob was doing.

"It's not us she's after," he yelled. "She's stealing STEALTH!"

Chapter 4
A STEALTHy situation

"At last!" snarled Jar-Wob. "I'm leaving this dried-up planet. I'm heading for Earth – and all those tasty humans! So much for Jack Slow and I-Wonder-Why Darkbrain; those inter-galactic twits aren't such hits!"

Jar-Wob grabbed hold of STEALTH's controls and revved the engine. "Up, up and away!" shrieked the vamp from Venus.

"I don't think so," said a voice.

"Who said that?" yelled Jar-Wob.

"I did," said STEALTH. "I'm a spaceship not a mobile blood bank. And I'm not taking an ugly old thing like you anywhere."

"I command you!" wailed Jar-Wob. "You're just a stupid computer! You must do as I say or you will pay!"

"No," said STEALTH. "You're a bad poet and you don't even know it. I'm staying here."

Jar-Wob was frothing at the mouth. She aimed a curse at STEALTH's computer chip. "I'll put a spell on you, so you must do whatever I tell you to do," she howled.

"You've got bats in your belfry, gran," said STEALTH. "You'd better get off my deck because this game won't be neck and neck."

STEALTH was enjoying itself. It had belonged to Jack long enough to learn all his bad jokes.

"How dare you!" said Jar-Wob.

"Please don't turn the other cheek," said STEALTH, "it's just as ugly."

Jar-Wob went very quiet. "If you don't take me where I want to go," she growled, "I shall break my magic mirror – then your dear Darkwit will be lost forever."

Without another word, Jar-Wob had grabbed hold of the controls and STEALTH had no choice but to take off.

Soon Venus was just a bright spot in the sky as STEALTH hurtled towards Earth.

"So many on Earth I'd like to meet – and every one a tasty treat!" laughed Jar-Wob.

Chapter 5

No fangs!

"Good old STEALTHy," whispered Jack. "It kept Jar-Wob talking long enough for me to climb on board!"

"Yes," agreed Wanda, "but it's going to take ages to un-programme all those bad jokes."

Jack looked serious. "I don't know how we're going to stop that Venusian vamp," said Jack. "She's got STEALTH and she's got your laser."

"I've got an idea," said Wanda. "One that will make her reflect on her bad behaviour."

"No fear! I'm all ears," said Jack.

Wanda groaned. Now Jack was talking in rhyme as well. It must be catching.

Jack crept quietly along the corridor to STEALTH's flight deck. The timing was important if Wanda's plan was going to work.

But he couldn't wait long – STEALTH was getting close to Earth.

Jar-Wob was looking in the mirror on the wall and combing her long, green hair.

"Mirror, mirror on the wall, who is the fairest of them all?" sang Jar-Wob in a creaky voice.

"Not you, you old battle-axe," snapped Wanda.

"What?!" shrieked Jar-Wob. "How did this meddling mortal and this ailing alien get on board? Well, it's a chance too good to pass, they'll soon be through the looking glass!"

She aimed a curse at Jack. Just at the right moment, he held up his pocket mirror.

Jar-Wob's curse bounced off the mirror and was reflected back at her.

With a puff of green smoke and a wail like a Martian banshee, she disappeared into the mirror.

Wanda leapt out of the mirror and landed on the floor with a thud, followed by the curtains and the sagging sofa.

Jar-Wob was trapped in the mirror, howling and wailing and spitting curses.

Jack grabbed both mirrors and threw them as hard as he could.

The mirrors shattered, breaking into hundreds of glittering pieces.

"Now that vampire has to retire!" said Wanda.

"Yeah," laughed Jack. "No fangs for the memory!"

Facts about vampires

The first vampire story in English was published in 1819 by John Polidori. His friend, Mary Shelley, wrote 'Frankenstein' in 1818.

The most famous vampire is 'Dracula'. Bram Stoker wrote this story in 1897.

Dracula was based on a real person, Vlad the Impaler. Vlad was a ruler in Romania in the 1430s. He impaled enemies on long sticks called 'stakes'.

The word 'dracul' means 'dragon' or 'devil' in Romanian. Don't tell Draco Malfoy!

You can kill a vampire with sunshine, fire, driving a stake through its heart, or cutting off its head. Or do all four at the same time!

People were writing about vampires over 1,000 years ago, although the idea is much, much older.

Vampire bats live in South America. They really do drink blood!

The series of vampire stories, 'Twilight', by Stephanie Meyer have sold over 116 million copies.

Jack's joke

What kind of ships do vampires sail?

Blood vessels!

Questions

Why is Wanda annoyed with Jack?

How did she get trapped in the mirror?

Where does Jar-Wob live?

How is Jar-Wob different from other vampires you've read about?

Why does Jar-Wob really want Jack to come to Venus?

How does STEALTH delay Jar-Wob taking off?

How does Jar-Wob make STEALTH take her to Earth?

What happens when Jar-Wob tries to curse Jack into the mirror?

How does Jack make sure that Jar-Wob can't come back?

Who makes the worst rhyme in the story?